Everyone Knows It

Prison drama set in London

Jacqueline Panton

Copyright © 2022 Jacqueline Panton

All rights reserved, including the right to reproduce this book, or portions thereof in any form. No part of this text may be reproduced, transmitted, downloaded, decompiled, reverse engineered, or stored, in any form or introduced into any information storage and retrieval system, in any form or by any means, whether electronic or mechanical without the express written permission of the author.

This is a work of fiction. Names and characters are the product of the author's imagination and any resemblance to actual persons, living or dead, is entirely coincidental.

The right of Jacqueline J Panton to be identified as author of this work has been asserted in accordance with sections 77 and 78 of the Copyright, Designs and Patents Act 1988.

A CIP catalogue record of this title is available from the British Library.

Everyone knows it.

Jacqueline Panton

Scene 1

The scene is set in the main prison block. Two men stand in the centre of the main wings. One of the men is an inmate known as Rush and the other a prison officer called Mr Gepps. Rush is eager to know what happened to a parcel he was expecting.

RUSH: Well.

MR. GEPPS: Well what?

RUSH: Come on.

MR. GEPPS: Come on what?

RUSH: Come on man, what's come in?

MR. GEPPS: I don't know what's come in.

RUSH: What's wrong with you man.

MR.GEPPS: There's nothing wrong with me.

RUSH: What's come in?

MR. GEPPS: I don't know do I.

RUSH: Ok……..

Everyone knows it.

Jacqueline Panton

Rush leaves Mr Gepps standing in the centre and walks onto one of the wings. He walks up some stairs to the second landing where he sees Mac. Mac is an inmate sometimes referred to as Soldier. He is also keen to hear about the parcel.

RUSH: 'e pisses me off!

MAC: What's up?

RUSH: 'e really pisses me off.

MAC: You know what e's like.

RUSH: I don't trust him.

MAC: Who does?

RUSH: I really don't rust him soldier.

MAC: Look, just let things rest for now, you don't wanna aggravate him.

RUSH: I swear.

MAC: I know.

The men stand on the second landing looking down on the lower floor.

RUSH: How much do you think came in?

MAC: Boy..........I dunno.

Everyone knows it.

Jacqueline Panton

RUSH: Two and a half no doubt.

MAC: No idea.

RUSH: No less than two.

MAC: I dunno.

RUSH: Boy.............

Rush and Mac stand on the landing in silence. As they stand looking down onto the lower floor, they see Mr Gepps talking to Gary, a mutual acquaintance.

RUSH: I don't believe it.

MAC: Don't even move!

RUSH: I don't fuckin believe it.

MAC: I'm warnin you Rush.

RUSH: I'm cool' I'm cool.

MAC: Now move back, don't let him see you.

RUSH: I'll kill him if..........

MAC: Move back man.

Gary looks up quickly, his eyes scanning the landing. Mr Gepps also looks up. They stand looking up for a while and then continue to talk to each other quietly as though not to be over-heard.

Everyone knows it.

Jacqueline Panton

RUSH: 'e's got money for me.

MAC: 'e's got money for everyone.

RUSH: 'e's got loads for me.

MAC: And he doesn't like to pay.

RUSH: 'e'd better pay soldier, I swear.

MAC: Just take it steady. When it comes to Gary, you have to study him......and then trap him.

An officer calls out 'All behind your doors,' and all the inmates start walking along the landings to their cells. Rush sees Gary walking back to his cell, he touches Mac and walks away from him. Walking up behind Gary he calls out to him.

RUSH: 'eh, what you sayin?

GARY: What?

RUSH: Don't what me. You know what I mean.

GARY: What are you talkin about!

RUSH: You know what I'm talkin about.

GARY: Hello.........I'm in prison.

RUSH: I don't care where you are.

GARY: Hello..............Where am I supposed to get it.

Everyone knows it.

Jacqueline Panton

RUSH: Blood, I want my money.

GARY: Blood....

RUSH: Don't play me.

GARY: I'm not playin you.

RUSH: Don't play me, don't try it.

GARY: Low me bruv

RUSH: This is not a lowin game.

GARY: I'll sort you out, you know I can't go nowhere.

RUSH: Yeh you do that.

GARY: I hear you.

RUSH: Nice.

Gary walks away from Rush. He walks down the landing to his cell. Rush stands on the landing in silence, he watches Gary as he walks down the landing until he disappears into his cell. Music can be heard in the background.

End of first scene

Everyone knows it.
Jacqueline Panton

Scene 2

Two men stand at the entrance to the officers Tea Room. Rush is desperate to find out what Peter, the Tea Boy, knows about anything that has come in.

RUSH: Have you got your stuff yet?

PETER: Nah. I've been waiting for properties almost two weeks now.

RUSH: I've got to get my stuff now, I need to.

PETER: Good luck, I've tried that one.

RUSH: Have you heard anythin?

PETER: Like what?

RUSH: Like what's come in.

PETER: Oh..... no

RUSH: It's quiet, but it's there.

PETER: Oh

RUSH: Nice too.

Rush leans on the door and stares hard at Peter. Peter appears nervous but begins to probe.

Everyone knows it.
Jacqueline Panton

PETER: Who knows?

RUSH: Most of 'em.

PETER: Like who?

RUSH: Most of 'em. Everyone who should know.

PETER: Maybe not a good thing.

RUSH: Maybe not a good thing.

PETER: Who's brought it in?

RUSH: Oh......crooked screw.........Gepp or somethin.

PETER: Oh I know who it is.

RUSH: 'e's well crooked, you cant trust him.

PETER: I know who you mean.

RUSH: 'e stitched my mate up before.

PETER: What did he do?

RUSH: Called the screws down on him.

PETER: What for?

RUSH: Sellin to some geezer.

PETER: What, the geezer grass him up?

Everyone knows it.

Jacqueline Panton

RUSH: Nah, Gepp didn't like the geezer.

PETER: Punk!

RUSH: Tell me about it, he's really petty

PETER: Just a minute.

Peter walks down the landing to his cell and Rush is left on his own. Rush leans over the railings and scans the landing below. He then makes a quick move out of sight. When Peter returns to the landing, Rush has disappeared and Bunny, an associate is walking on the landing.

BUNNY: Waa gwaan.

PETER: So so, you know.

BUNNY: Where everybody at?

PETER: I dunno.

BUNNY: So............ what's the chat?

PETER: Something in but no-one knows.

BUNNY: Someone knows.

PETER: Well you know how it goes.

BUNNY: Rush should know, he always knows.

PETER: Nah...............doubt it.

Everyone knows it.

Jacqueline Panton

BUNNY: He knows.

PETER: I dunno.

BUNNY: Ok..........you aint talkin.

Bunny nods his head and walks away from Peter. Pete remains standing on the landing. As he stands there, he feels a tap on his shoulder. He turns around to see Rush.

RUSH: I saw him comin.

PETER: You could of warned me.

RUSH: Not enough time mate.

PETER: He wants to know everything.

RUSH: 'e's a snake.

PETER: Right! It's the way he goes about it.

RUSH: 'e know what 'e's doin.

PETER: He was right in my face and I was like........

RUSH: That's how he moves, e's trouble.

PETER: He was in my face tryin to drill me asking me about the stuff and who knows.

RUSH: Did he talk about me?

PETER: Yeh, he reckons you know.

Everyone knows it.

Jacqueline Panton

RUSH: 'e's a punk, always wants to know peoples business.

PETER: He reckons you know everything.

RUSH: 'e can reckon all he likes, I aint tellin im nothin.

PETER: He's dangerous you know.

RUSH: I know 'e's dangerous, 'e's a coward though, 'e can't stand up for himself either, 'e always uses some other youth.

PETER: That's why he's dangerous.

RUSH: 'e will never front anything by imself.

PETER: That's why he's dangerous.

RUSH: But 'e needs to watch them same youth dere.

PETER: They're dumb.

RUSH: They can switch on im anytime.

Peter follows Rush into his cell. They sit smoking for a long while, and music can be head in the background. Then Peter notices that Rush is reading something.

PETER: What are you doing?

RUSH: Just chillin, reading a letter from my friend. 'e's been through a lot you know.

Everyone knows it.

Jacqueline Panton

PETER: Like what?

RUSH: 'e's been through some mad stuff.

PETER: Mad stuff?

RUSH: Well, his sister had some mad things done to 'er in Africa I think...... I couldn't read it properly.

PETER: Mad things done to her?

RUSH: yeah, sexual stuff like, like when she was young, the people in 'er villiage sewed up 'er private part.

PETER: What do you mean?

RUSH: They sewed up her private part.

PETER: Why did they do that?

RUSH: I dunno. er parents allowed it, and she's been in pain ever since.

PETER: Is she still sewn up?

RUSH: Well yes, it's just like when you have stitches I guess, when the sewing falls out, your flesh is welded together.

PETER: My oh my, that's MAD!

RUSH: I'm tellin ya.

PETER: So your friend took it to heart?

Everyone knows it.

Jacqueline Panton

RUSH: 'e's bitter about it because ... something that 'e said in the letter, I couldn't read it properly. She went a bit mad and I think they tried to kill 'er.

PETER: These Africans can do some mad things.

RUSH: I'm tellin ya

PETER: What's it all about? Why do they need to do that?

RUSH: Dunno. 'e said some more mad things but I couldn't read it properly.

PETER: Why couldn't you read it properly?

RUSH: I just couldn't. I could read bits but not all of it properly.

Peter sits quietly for a short while. He appears to be thinking. Then he speaks.

PETER: Well I better go, go and see what my man is up to. Later.

RUSH: Yeah-yeah later.

Peter is leaning over the railings on the third floor. Doc, an inmate known as Doctors Orders, looks up from the second floor and sees him. Doc climbs the stairs and approaches him.

DOC: You cool

PETER: Yeah yeah

Everyone knows it.

Jacqueline Panton

DOC: Just checking that everyone's alright y'know.

PETER: Everything's cool, could do with some more of course but that's everyone's story.

DOC: Well you know how that goes, gotta pay for everything in this world. Thought I'd seen Rush up here still.

PETER: He's around you know, I've just seen him. He was reading a letter.

DOC: Can he read though?

PETER: Why you say that?

DOC: Just. I notice him still.

PETER: Funny.

DOC: What?

PETER: Funny you should say that.

DOC: Why, you notice?

PETER: Yeah.

DOC: I notice long time.

PETER: Me too, but I don't make a big thing.

DOC: He can't read at all star.

Everyone knows it.
Jacqueline Panton

PETER: I dunno.

DOC: He's got issues I know, but he don't talk. He can't read trust me.

PETER: I dunno, it's just that he was reading something and he just kept on saying that he couldn't read it properly. He didn't really want to talk about it either.

DOC: What was he reading about?

PETER: Some woman in Africa had her private part sewn up. Some religious thing or something.

DOC: Oh, no, that's called..... what's it called again? Ah, Female Genital Mutation.

End of second scene

Everyone knows it.

Jacqueline Panton

Scene 3

The prisoners are on 'association' sometimes known as 'free-time'. Digo, sometimes referred to as 'Prophet', walks into Rush's cell. Rush is sitting on his bed listening to music. Digo knows about the parcel and wants to know what Rush knows, but Rush has decided to keep-a-low.

DIGO: Many come and many fall.

RUSH: What you talkin bout now.

DIGO: Many come and many fall.

RUSH: It won't happen this time.

DIGO: Why not?

RUSH: Top screw.

DIGO: 'e's not a top screw, 'e's a crooked screw.

RUSH: 'e can hold it down.

DIGO: Yeh, by any means necessary.

RUSH: It's what you gotta do prophet. You're either doin it or you're not doin it.

Everyone knows it.

Jacqueline Panton

DIGO: I don't see it workin.

RUSH: 'ow's that?

DIGO: Too many on.

RUSH: Screws?

DIGO: Nah, man.

RUSH: Few idiots, that don't mean none.

DIGO: Only takes few idiots.

Rush, realising that Digo wants to chat, decides to try a quick probe. He rises from his bed and turns off the music.

RUSH: What wing?

DIGO: 'B' Wing.

RUSH: For sure?

DIGO: For sure.

RUSH: How much?

DIGO: Five ks.

RUSH: Swear down?

DIGO: Swear down.

RUSH: Who's movin it?

Everyone knows it.

Jacqueline Panton

DIGO: Hench-man, small time but pushin through.

RUSH: When?

DIGO: Free-time.

RUSH: Boy.............

DIGO: There's no other time.

RUSH: Boy...........I don't get much free time, bad rep you know.

DIGO: You got nuff man though.

RUSH: True dat.

Digo is distracted by a noise outside of the cell and rushes out to see what it's all about. Whilst he is out, Doc, a man referred to as 'Doctors Orders', passes by and sees Rush's cell door open. He walks into the cell. Music is being played on a low volume.

DOC: What's gwaanin.

RUSH: So so you know. What does the doctor order?

DOC: So......so.........what you need?

RUSH: What you got?

DOC: Well.......now.

RUSH: What you got?

Everyone knows it.
Jacqueline Panton

DOC: What you need?

RUSH: Come on man.

DOC: I got what you need not what you think you need.

RUSH: I…………need some stock.

DOC: You know I got dat.

RUSH: How much we talkin?

DOC: I got stock man.

Doc reaches into his sock and pulls out something wrapped in what looked like cling film. He hands it to Rush.

DOC: Hold that.

RUSH: Nice.

DOC: Don't tell me you aint heard we come in.

RUSH: I heard.

DOC: We come in man, nice too.

As they talk, a familiar voice is heard outside the cell. Both men freeze as they listen to the voice. It is the voice of Mellow, a street soldier. He is shouting to another inmate who is standing on the landing of the third floor. Doc walks out of the cell to see what is going on. He sees Mellow, Mellow is shouting to the landing above Rush's cell.

Everyone knows it.

Jacqueline Panton

MELLOW: When I say somethin, memba I told ya.

DAN: Well, I never did doubt you, you know, I only said

MELLOW: Never mind man, jus memba.

DAN: It will have to start pushing soon, can't just be in one place, you know.

MELLOW: All under control man.

Mellow turns and walks along the isle to his cell. Dan is a brother who Doc doesn't like. He was also a street soldier. Was, is the word. He became known for his two-faced ways and was demoted by a drug lord. Dan's reputation preceded him and he was soon disliked by a lot of people. He is still standing on the landing looking down to the landing below. He sees Doc and Doc is looking at him. He stares down at Doc. Doc looks away and walks back into Rush's cell. Music is being played on a low volume.

DOC: Can't stand that brother you know.

RUSH: What brother?

DOC: The one talking to Mellow just now.

RUSH: I know who you mean.

DOC: Just something about him.

RUSH: I know what you mean.

DOC: He's a nasty piece of work.

Everyone knows it.

Jacqueline Panton

RUSH: I know just what you mean, that thing.

DOC: And he knows I don't like him.

RUSH: That's why you gotta be careful.

DOC: He's a pussy.

RUSH: Still.

Suddenly Digo walks into Rush's cell. He is singing 'The Harder They Come, The Harder They Fall', theme tune for the film, 'The Harder They Come. Rush realises that he is angry.

RUSH: What's wrong now?

DIGO: Boy.........I don't even want to say anythin.

RUSH: What's up?

DIGO: Boy..........I don't even want to bother sayin.

RUSH: It's that same brother Dan isn't it.

DIGO: How you know?

RUSH: I know man.

DOC: You and me both man, he's a pussy.

DIGO: I'm a person, I don't mess about.

Everyone knows it.
Jacqueline Panton

DOC: He's a pussy, he can't make a move.

DIGO: 'e's standin on the landin and I want to get by.

DOC: He's good at starting things.

DIGO: 'e's standin on the landin and I want to get by and he knows I want to get by.

DOC: He wouldn't move.

DIGO: 'e wouldn't move.

RUSH: 'e searches for trouble.

DIGO: 'e wouldn't move, swear down, lookin me in the eye an all.

DOC: I know just what he needs, just what he needs. He needs the right person.

RUSH: 'e won't 'ave to look too far.

Rush starts singing along to a reggae song that can be heard in the background, and is joined by Digo and Doc. The song is as follows;

'Dem nuh nice, dem nasty

da-da-da da da da da

'Dem nuh nice, dem nast-ee

Everyone knows it.
Jacqueline Panton

da-da-da da da da da

'Dem nuh nice, dem nasty

da-da-da da da da da

da da da da da da da.

End of the third scene.

Everyone knows it.

Jacqueline Panton

Scene 4

Digo is sitting on the bed in his cell smoking. He is thinking about his next move as stock is getting low. Suddenly he looks up at his open cell door and sees Bunny standing in the doorway.

DIGO: Well?

BUNNY: Come on man.

DIGO: Come on what, bout come on.

BUNNY: Hard runnins man.

DIGO: Hard times.

BUNNY: It's not easy blood.

Both men are silent for a few minutes. Digo stares hard at Bunny as he smokes his roll-up. Bunny stares back at him. Digo decides to break the silence.

DIGO: Step inside man, don't be hoggin up my door.

BUNNY: You know I work man.

DIGO: I need results star.

Everyone knows it.
Jacqueline Panton

BUNNY: You'll get results star.

DIGO: When?

BUNNY: Look, I can't hold him down yet.

DIGO: 'e's around all the time blood.

BUNNY: Not when 'e sees me.

DIGO: So what's 'e sayin?

BUNNY: Well....'e aint talkin.

DIGO: Aint talking won't do.

BUNNY: Man wants to know what man is dealin with man.

DIGO: Aint talkin won't do man.

BUNNY: 'e'll talk.

DIGO: 'e makes tea for them, he knows somethin.

BUNNY: 'e'll talk.

DIGO: They're a bunch of pussies man, even I could drill them.

BUNNY: You're welcome. I said he'll talk alright!

Bunny walks out of the cell leaving Digo sitting on his bed. He is angry because he feels that Digo doesn't have any faith in him. He makes his way up to the 'tea room' and

Everyone knows it.
Jacqueline Panton

stands outside. On the landing above Mellow can be heard calling out to Gary.

MELLOW: I don't chase star.

GARY: Don't chase then.

MELLOW: I won't, I'm waitin.

GARY: You've got no choice.

MELLOW: You're gettin bright I see.

GARY: Not bright just real.

MELLOW: Well, how about comin up with the real ting.

GARY: Look if you can't wait, it's not my fault.

MELLOW: He's told you what's going on.

GARY: No he hasn't.

MELLOW: Don't play me blood.

GARY: Blood.

MELLOW: That's not what I heard still.

Their voices can no longer be heard. Bunny walks inside the 'tea room' and sees Peter sitting down in an armchair drinking a cup of tea.

BUNNY: It's alright for some.

Everyone knows it.

Jacqueline Panton

PETER: Meaning?

BUNNY: It's alright for some.

PETER: Well, you know.

BUNNY: No I don't, but I want to.

PETER: Ok.

BUNNY: I need to know and I want to.

PETER: Ok........just what are we talking about.

BUNNY: You know what we're talkin about.

PETER: No I don't.

BUNNY: Yes you do.

PETER: No I don't.

BUNNY: Look........

PETER: Look what?

BUNNY: I'm under pressure here.

PETER: What pressure, from who?

BUNNY: Pressure man, I'm under pressure.

PETER: Look what's this gotta do with me?

Everyone knows it.
Jacqueline Panton

BUNNY: Well, I think you know where I'm comin from.

PETER: I'm not in your mix up man.

BUNNY: Oh, it's not my mix up.

PETER: Well it's not mine.

Bunny walks right up to Peter who is still sitting in the armchair and stares hard at him. He speaks to him in a low voice.

BUNNY: You're dissin me!

PETER: What?

BUNNY: You heard.

Peter puts down his cup of tea and jumps to his feet.

PETER: You wanna to diss me?

BUNNY: I don't have a problem.

PETER: You wanna to diss me?

BUNNY: I don't have a problem.

The two men stand face to face staring at each other in silence. They stand there for a while. Bunny breaks the silence.

BUNNY: Man asks you a simple thing and you can't answer.

Everyone knows it.

Jacqueline Panton

PETER: What thing is that?

BUNNY: You're giving me the run-arounds man.

PETER: I'm giving you the run-arounds?

BUNNY: Well, yes, I ask you a simple question.

PETER: Simple question, what was that?

BUNNY: I asked you a question but it's like.

PETER: What question was that?

BUNNY: I asked you a question but it's like you're hidin somethin.

PETER: I aint hidin nothin.

BUNNY: A simple question and it's like you're hidin.

PETER: I aint got nothing to hide.

Bunny moves away from Peter allowing him to breathe. Peter doesn't move.

BUNNY: It's just that, well, everyone's hungry and.

PETER: Everyone's hungry, I know that.

BUNNY: I know you know that but.

PETER: I know that everyone's hungry but it's one thing to be hungry and another thing to try and distress man.

Everyone knows it.
Jacqueline Panton

BUNNY: I'm not distressin man. It's gonna benefit man.

PETER: Yea, how? How is it gonna benefit man?

BUNNY: I always feed out so don't try it.

PETER: You never fed me.

BUNNY: Stop that.

PETER: You never fed me.

BUNNY: So you say.

PETER: So I mean.

BUNNY: Anyway I know that nuff man pretend they don't eat.

PETER: Not this man.

BUNNY: Anyway.

Bunny walks over to the wall, leans against it and folds his arms. He stands there looking at Peter for a while. Just then Mr. Gepps walks into the 'tea room'. Bunny feels uneasy but tries to look relaxed.

PETER: How many cuppas?

MR. GEPPS: Just do three.

PETER: Three it is.

Everyone knows it.
Jacqueline Panton

BUNNY: Er………so later then Tea.

PETER: Laters.

Bunny looks at Peter and then walks out of the 'tea room'.

End of fourth scene.

Everyone knows it.

Jacqueline Panton

Scene 5

Mr Gepps and DIigo are in the SO's office on the third floor. Mr Gepps is sitting in an armchair. Digo is standing by his desk

MR GEPPS: How's it going?

DIGO: It's cool, it's cool.

MR GEPPS: Got enough?

DIGO: Cool, cool for now anyway.

MR GEPPS: My man not giving you trouble is he?

DIGO: Well, you know how it goes. I just don't like the way he was brought in. It was just so quick and undercover if you ask me. Plus there's the fact that we don't get on.

MR GEPPS: Well you know how it goes, he's not a nice guy but I know you can work with him.

DIGO: I'll just have to see how it goes.

Just then Taylor, a senior officer, enters the office. He stops in his tracks and looks at Digo, then looks over at Mr

Everyone knows it.
Jacqueline Panton

Gepps. Mr Gepps nods his head slightly and Taylor takes a seat in the office.

MR GEPPS: All clear.

Taylor sits looking at Mr Gepps. He says nothing.

MR GEPPS: Ah.... it's safe....really.

DIGO: I better get goin. Later.

Digo nods to Taylor as he leaves. Taylor ignores him and stares at Mr Gepps.

TAYLOR: What you doin?

MR GEPPS: Listen..............

TAYLOR: What you doin?

MR GEPPS: Look, I know this one.

TAYLOR: You know this one? You don't know anyone.

MR GEPPS: Calm down, I've got it under control. He does as he's told and he gets what he wants. Sorted.

TAYLOR: I've heard this before and I'm warnin you. When my life is on the line....so is yours.....and everyone else.

MR GEPPS: Look he's worked for me before and I've had no problems. It's when you start dealing with people you don't know. That when trouble starts.

Everyone knows it.
Jacqueline Panton

TAYLOR: Look, all I'm sayin is, I'm doing this for money, not for trouble, so be careful who you expose me to. I don't care what they want, they always want, that's why they're in 'ere. One minute they're alright, the next minute they're going behind your back and talkin to some other wrong'en. I don't care what you do but I don't like Digo, he's sly, he can't be trusted and he doesn't like screws. Remember that.

MR GEPPS: He's delivered for you before.

TAYLOR: Not for me! It was Dan I used. Don't like him either but you know where you stand with him. I don't like any of em.

MR GEPPS: Well... I'm just gonna work with who I've got. I've no choice really. I can trust him and that's what matters.

Just then another officer referred to as Parks, comes into the office. He nods to Taylor. Taylor acknowledges him with a nod. Parks sits down and stares back but says nothing.

TAYLOR: We've just been havin a little chat.

PARKS: Really.........

TAYLOR: I've told him where I stand.....and where 'e stands.

PARKS: Think it'll work?

TAYLOR: Well.........we'll see.

Everyone knows it.

Jacqueline Panton

PARKS: That's true.

MR GEPPS: Look, stop blaming me for the cock-up!

PARKS: Why?

MR GEPPS: Stop blaming me!

PARKS: Why should we stop blaming you? Give us a good reason.

MR GEPPS: Because it wasn't my cock-up!

PARKS: Whose cock-up was it?

MR GEPPS: I wasn't mine!

PARKS: Whose was it then? Who made the arrangements?

MR GEPPS: I made the arrangements and no-one could stick to them.

PARKS: Oh no...You made the arrangements and two officers got fired STICKING TO THEM!

MR GEPPS: That's a lie and you know it.

PARKS: It's the truth and you know it.

MR GEPPS: I'm not going to argue with you. You're only on my back because I kept my job.

PARKS: That's right.

Everyone knows it.

Jacqueline Panton

TAYLOR: Look this is goin to get us nowhere. Cut the crap and get on with it. We all know what we're doin, so let's do it. We're on a time thing here, we haven't got much time. This thing has got to get to where it's gotta get to and quick too. All I've got to say is this....if I get fucked...... I'm not goin alone.

MR GEPPS: I hear that.

TAYLOR: But do you hear it. I hope so. For your sake.

MR GEPPS: I said I hear that.

End of fifth scene

Everyone knows it.

Jacqueline Panton

Scene 6

It is time for 'association'. The men have been unlocked and are now leaving their cells. Digo has come out of his cell and is standing on the landing on the third floor. He leans over the railings and looks down to the ground floor. He sees Parks climbing the stairs from the ground floor. He watches him until he reaches the third floor. Parks stands by the stairs and turns to look at Digo. He stares at him for a while and then walks slowly towards him on the landing.

PARKS: No leaning over the railings, you know that.

DIGO attempts to walk away.

PARKS: Er, by the way I er spoke to Gepps and he reckons you're quite a soldier.

DIGO freezes but says nothing.

PARKS: I'm not after anything.

DIGO is quiet for a while and then he speaks.

DIGO: What d'you want then?

PARKS: Like I said, I want nothing, I was just saying, I had a little chat with Gepps and he said that you were willing to get things moving. I mean, don't know how true it is.......

Everyone knows it.
Jacqueline Panton

DIGO: Boy.... I got nothin to say.

PARKS: Like I said, I want nothing. I just thought you might be interested.

Digo freezes again but after a while begins to probe.

DIGO: Interested in what?

PARKS: Well now....... depends.

DIGO: On?

PARKS: Well..........it depends.

DIGO: Depends on what?

Parks is silent for a while, he looks around the landing and scans down below then looks straight at Digo.

PARKS: It depends on what you want.

DIGO: I need more than that.

PARKS: You need more than what?

DIGO: I need more than 'it depends o what you want'. What's on offer?

PARKS: Well.........A few things are on offer.

DIGO: I'm waiting.....

Everyone knows it.

Jacqueline Panton

PARKS: Hang on.... I don't know much about you......Apart from what Gepps told me.

DIGO: What more do you want to know?

PARKS: What have you done for Gepps?

DIGO: What d'you mean?

PARKS: Well....What was the deal? Why does he think you're a soldier?

DIGO: Hang on, why am I tellin you?

PARKS: Well, you don't have to tell me anything. I just wanted to know something about what you're capable of. If I make an offer, I like to know who I'm offering to. You seem alright but I just wanna know, y'know.

DIGO: If I'm dealin with someone, I like to deal straight. I'm init for the money but I like to give respect and get respect in return.

PARKS: I got no problem with that, I'm the same. You say you're in it for the money. How much money?

DIGO: My fair share.

PARKS: How much are we talking?

DIGO: Come on man.

PARKS: What if I could make your share bigger?

Everyone knows it.

Jacqueline Panton

Digo is silent, he stands looking at Parks. Parks stares hard at Digo for a while and then breaks the silence.

PARKS: What if I could double your money?

DIGO: Ooooh.....Now what are we talkin about 'ere?

Parks is silent but stands staring hard at Digo. Digo stares back and raises his eyebrows.

DIGO: What is it about me that makes people try it with me? I don't play games man.

PARKS: Play games? Who's playing games? I make offers, I don't play games.

DIGO; You mean it don't ya...

PARKS: I said I make offers, I don't play games.

Both men are quiet for a few minutes. They continue to stare at each other, then they both speak at the same time.

PARKS/DIGO: Ok.

They are quiet again and then they both attempt to speak again.

PARKS/DIGO: Ok.

They both laugh and then PARKS quickly speaks.

PARKS: Ok, let me guess, Gepps has given you some food to push around.

Everyone knows it.

Jacqueline Panton

Digo says nothing. He stares at Parks and then quickly nods his head. Parks continues.

PARKS: He's given you about roughly 10k

Digo says nothing. His eyes are fixed on Parks as Parks waits for confirmation. Parks continues.

PARKS: Between 10 and 20k?

Digo says nothing. His eyes are still fixed on Parks. Parks takes a deep breath.

PARKS: Come on man, this is business.

Digo still says nothing for a while and then finally he speaks in a quiet voice.

DIGO: He's given me 15k

Parks stares at Digo. He's not sure that Digo is telling the truth. Digo continues.

DIGO: What can you do on that?

Parks looks hard at Digo for a while and then speaks.

PARKS: I don't believe you.

Digo is quiet; he stands there staring at Parks.

PARKS: I don't believe it. Somet's not right.

DIGO: What d'you mean?

Everyone knows it.
Jacqueline Panton

Parks is quiet, he stands there rubbing his beard and looking at Digo.

DIGO: What d'you mean something's not right?

PARKS: Well.......I dunno, I heard different.

Digo raises his eyebrows as he studies Parks.

DIGO: What did you hear?

PARKS: Well, first tell me who you're dealing with because I may have got this wrong.

DIGO: Dealin with?

PARKS: Who d'you sell to?

After pausing for a couple of minutes Digo decides to speak.

DIGO: It's well known, I deal with Bunny and Gary.....

PARKS: Bunny and Gary are on this?

DIGO: I didn't say that.

PARKS: You're sharing the food with Bunny and Gary?

DIGO: Somet like that. Why? Heard different?

PARKS: As I was saying I heard, contrary to what you're telling me, that 30k had gone out to the man. Now, I thought that man was you, until a moment ago.

Everyone knows it.

Jacqueline Panton

Both men stand looking at each other. None of them move for about 20 seconds. Parks breaks the silence.

PARKS: You know that Gepps doesn't trust Doc too much.

DIGO: Yeh yeh I know that.

PARKS But he does trust Dan. You know that don't you?

Digo freezes, his eyes fixed on Parks. Parks stands still, not saying a word.

DIGO: You're lyin, lyin through your teeth.

PARKS: Oh, I'm not lying. Dan is the man and Gepps is double crossing you.

Digo is still frozen; he stands there for a few seconds and then makes for the door.

PARKS: Where are you going?

DIGO: I gotta go.

PARKS: Where? Look think about this, don't rock the boat, you've got to be smart.

DIGO: I've gotta go, I've gotta see Doc.

PARKS: Ok.

DIGO: I had a funny feelin about all of this. I need to think about this.....And the money.

<u>*Everyone knows it.*</u>
Jacqueline Panton

PARKS: Sure. You really need to think about this and while you're thinking, think about double money. Ok?

Digo scratches his head.

DIGO: We'll see.

Digo leaves Parks standing on the landing. He descends to the ground floor and disappears.

End of sixth scene.

Everyone knows it.

Jacqueline Panton

Scene 7

Peter is in the tea room sitting in an armchair drinking a cup of tea. He hears a noise behind him and turns to see Digo.

DIGO: Whats up?

PETER: Ah Digo, whats up?

DIGO: Well you know how it goes, so so.

PETER: I'm just chillin y'know.

Digo is silent for a while, and then he speaks

DIGO: Have you seen Bunny lately?

Peter freezes for a while, and then he speaks.

PETER: Boy……. I don't even want to see that brother you know.

DIGO: I know, I heard. He can be a bit much sometimes. I'm always telling him to calm down.

PETER: You need to tell him some more…….I nearly knocked him out.

Everyone knows it.

Jacqueline Panton

DIGO: Tell me, I've nearly done that myself.

PETER: I mean…really knocked him out.

DIGO: I know.

Peter is quiet for a couple of minutes, and then he speaks.

PETER: He seemed to be sure I knew something.

Digo is silent for a while, and then he speaks.

DIGO: About what?

The room is silent for a moment.

PETER: About what's come in I'm sure……..but he's a fool.

DIGO: Why you say that?

PETER: Because he's a fool if he thinks I'd give him man's business to spread in the streets. You know what I mean?

The room is filled with silence for a few minutes. Then Peter swings his chair around so that his back is facing Digo. He turns on the radio and a song can be heard.

DIGO: Yeah, I know what you mean.

The room is again filled with silence for a few minutes, then Peter speaks.

Everyone knows it.

Jacqueline Panton

PETER: Just so it goes, you know.

The room is again filled with silence. Then digo speaks in a very soft voice.

DIGO: Yeah.

There is silence for about fifteen minutes. Peter turns around to find that Digo has quietly left the room. About thirty minutes have passed and Peter is still sitting quietly in the tea-room thinking. He is not allowed to have the door fully closed whilst in the tea-room by himself but he feels that it is too wide open. He gets up to close it in a little. As he pushes the door, it comes to a halt, he looks down to see Bunny's foot blocking the door.

BUNNY: On your own?

Peter responds trying to sound normal.

PETER: What?

Bunny pushes the door open so that Peter has to step back.

BUNNY: Are you by yourself?

PETER: Yeah, just chillin y'know.

There is an awkward silence as Peter sits down in his armchair.

BUNNY: Dont you get bored of makin tea all the time?

Everyone knows it.

Jacqueline Panton

Peter sighs and is silent for a few seconds.

PETER: Look, you want something dont you? You're not 'ere for nothin.

Bunny is not surprised but clears his throat before he speaks.

BUNNY: Ah…..yes I wanted to talk about the other day.

Peter straightens himself up in the armchair ready to listen. Bunny notices and continues to speak.

BUNNY: I was really wound up man, had a lot of pressure on me.

Peter sits quietly listening.

BUNNY: I had things I needed to do and there was a lot of pressure on me and….you just weren't givin.

Bunny stops speaking for a while and the room is silent. He begins to speak again.

BUNNY: You weren't givin nothin and you know I can lose my cool.

Peter sits up at this point and responds.

PETER: Yes you can lose your cool! And you do don't you.

Bunny is quiet for a couple of minutes, and then he speaks.

Everyone knows it.

Jacqueline Panton

BUNNY: Yes, I can lose my cool but you could have 'elped! You could've 'elped yuself Tea. You know that pressure is all around.

PETER: Yeah I know, but I don't like when you bring your shit to me.

BUNNY: I hear that. I hear that but you know still.

The pair sit in silence for a while and then Peter speaks.

PETER: What was it all about? I mean, what was it all about anyway?

Bunny thinks for a minute and then tries to answer Peter.

BUNNY: You know what it was about!

He catches himself.

BUNNY: I mean, you know where I'm comin from. Digo is a hard man you know, when he wants somethin, he can be a pain. He disrespect me nuff time but I still hold it down y'know.

He is silent for a second or two.

BUNNY: He's disrespected me a few times and that's not really a wise thing to do.

The room silent for a minute or two. Peter clears his throat and then he speaks.

PETER: Why do you say that?

Everyone knows it.

Jacqueline Panton

There is silence in the room. Bunny appears to be thinking for a couple of minutes, and then he looks at Peter.

BUNNY: He's not a wise guy y'know, because if he was, he wouldn't cut himself short.

PETER: What do you mean?

BUNNY: Cut himself short. He cuts himself short by cussin out the wrong people.

He pauses for a couple of minutes before he speaks again.

BUNNY: I know a lot he could benefit from. I know a lot of things he needs to know. He thinks he's the don in all of this, but he isn't and he needs to watch his back.

Peter looks at Bunny and remains silent for a while. Then he begins to probe a little.

PETER: Umm....really? Who d'you think the don is then?

Bunny looks at peter without saying a word for a few seconds. Then he speaks in a low voice.

BUNNY: You know better than that, come on.

Peter shrugs his shoulders and sits quietly for a couple of minutes. He begins to probe again.

PETER: Nah, seriously though.

The room is quiet for about five minutes. In this time, Bunny stares at Peter and Peter is staring back at Bunny.

Everyone knows it.
Jacqueline Panton

Bunny appears to be thinking hard in a distant stare. He decides to break the silence.

BUNNY: Let's just say, e's not.

Peter begins to tap the arm of his chair with his fingers. Only the tapping can be heard as the men sit in silence once again.

End of seventh scene.

Everyone knows it.
Jacqueline Panton

Scene 8

The scene opens with Dan sitting on a chair in a basement floor landing. Peter is sitting with him. This ground floor landing is part of a wing for vulnerable prisoners. Dan is helping as an orderly, whilst Peter can use his 'tea boy' status to get anywhere. It is the perfect place for them to meet.

PETER: These are the things man, that piss me off.

DAN: I hear dat still.

PETER: They're a bunch of pussies …. They all think it's going on for them, especially that Bunny. He'll get a shock one day …… him and that same Digo. They're a bunch of pussies.

DAN: I told you about them didn't I. I told you they're pussies' man. Memba the time when they was all involved in the big shit.

PETER: Ah…. The big shit! They all went on like they didn't know anything. I was like ………… shocked.

DAN: I hear dat still.

PETER: I was just … shocked, because they put themselves over so real, and …….

Everyone knows it.

Jacqueline Panton

Dan cuts in as Peter goes into thought.

DAN: Yes! That was the thing. They put themselves over so real and all the time, they were setting man up.

PETER: That's right. Setting man up.

They are both quiet for a few seconds and then they both speak together.

PETER/DAN: All the one name Rush!

They look at each other and laugh, then Peter continues to speak.

PETER: Rush is a dog man. It's hard to detect, but he's a dog.

DAN: He helped to set me up as far as I'm concerned. He reckons he was not involved but he got near to read the situation.

PETER: Read the situation! Well he got too near.

DAN: He said he was reading them up.

PETER: Don't believe that at all. If he was reading them up. He's crap at it, but I guess it's still better than what he can do on paper.

Dan says nothing. Peter pauses for a while, then continues.

PETER: He can't read y'know.

Everyone knows it.

Jacqueline Panton

Dan looks at Peter for a while, smiles but still says nothing. Peter notices and changes the subject.

PETER: Memba when we was on the road back in the day?

DAN: Tell me man, those were the days.

PETER: Me and you always knew where we stood with each other. It was funny how it worked.

DAN: It was like we could read each other's mind.

PETER: Same thing I was gonna say.

DAN: I didn't feel like I had to question your loyalty.

PETER: That's right.

DAN: There was just this …… silent thing between us.

PETER: Tell me about it …….. I know.

They both sit there for a while thinking about back in the day. They sit there thinking for a while and then Peter speaks.

PETER: So what's happening about the gear then?

Dan freezes for a moment, then speaks as though he was trying to remember something.

DAN: Oh …. right … the thing … Gepps has got that you know. He's moving kinda weird though … He talks to

Everyone knows it.
Jacqueline Panton

everyone and if he doesn't like you, well …. He can be nasty. He's very twofaced as well. You've got to watch him.

PETER: He's very twofaced. He's dangerous. He needs to be careful who he deals with. … man will kill each other.

DAN: He's got Rush hasn't he?

PETER: Yep.

Dan is quiet for while, then speaks.

DAN: What does Rush know though?

PETER: Well …. Not much really, he just know he's due to get some.

Both Dan and Peter sit in silence for a minute. Dan is looking at Peter, and Peter is looking at the ground. Dan speaks quietly.

DAN: We need to see this Gepps, you and me both. We need to pin him down and let him know the real score.

PETER: Yep.

There is silence for a few minutes then they both stand up as if reading each other's mind and walk towards the stairs. Dan grabs a newspaper from a Poole table as he passes it. He speaks again.

DAN: I'm not going to be messed about this time ….. it might boil down to me and him.

Everyone knows it.

Jacqueline Panton

PETER: I hear dat.

They both climb the stairs to find Gepps standing at the gate with his keys in his hand. He opens the gate and lets the men onto the wings.

PETER: Later man.

DAN: Yeah yeah.

Dan climbs the stairs to the third landing. He goes into his cell and pull out a chair and sits on it outside his cell door. He begins to read the newspaper. He glances up and sees Gary walking towards him.

GARY: What's goin on blood?

DAN: Going on? What d'you mean?

GARY: Everyone knows star!

DAN: Everyone knows about what?

GARY: About you and Gepps it seems.

Gary stops talking and scans the landing quickly.

DAN: How d'you mean?

GARY: Mellow is runnin me down asking if Gepps has told me. What's that about?

Everyone knows it.
Jacqueline Panton

DAN: Ah……. Mellow, don't worry about him. You don't need to tell him anything, you're dealing with me. Just avoid him if you can…… to be honest.

GARY: I just don't like the way he comes onto me. He's a bully and there is a man for them.

DAN: Really……… man …like who?

GARY: Never mind. There's a man for them.

Gary scans the landing again and begins to walk away from Dan.

GARY: Well ……yeah …… alright, later.

Dan watches as he disappears. He turns his head in the opposite direction and sees Taylor approaching him. He tries to look busy and continues reading the newspaper. Taylor slows down but continues to walk towards him.

TAYLOR: How's it going then?

Dan looks up from his newspaper and stares hard at Taylor for at least a minute. He then speaks.

DAN: As well as can be expected, y'know.

TAYLOR: Saw that idiot talkin to you earlier, they one who works for Digo. You wanna keep away from that one, they all belong to Gepps.

Dan is pensive for a minute and sits still. He then speaks.

Everyone knows it.

Jacqueline Panton

DAN: Like you said, he was talking to me.

TAYLOR: Yes, he was .... I've waited a long time for this to come in, and nothin could be worse than losin it to idiots ...... Y'know what I mean?

Dan stares at Taylor for a good thirty seconds without blinking. He then looks back down at his newspaper. Taylor continues to speak.

TAYLOR: I don't want to go on but, people like that are scum. They have no respect for anyone. They only think about themselves. They would double-cross anyone, and you know he's a crackhead, right?

Dan looks up once more from reading his newspaper and stares at Taylor hard for about a minute. Taylor continues to speak.

TAYLOR: He's a crackhead and he talks too much. When he gets desperate, he talks. He ate out of bins in the street for fuck sake. You need to watch that guy, he'll double-cross you, and if he double-crosses you, he'll double-cross me..... if he double-crosses me .... That won't be good for any of us.

Dan looks up sharply at Taylor. Staring at him without blinking, he speaks.

DAN: What d'you mean?

TAYLOR: Well, like I said, I don't want you talkin to, or dealin with anyone who can hurt me.

Everyone knows it.

Jacqueline Panton

At this point, Dan not only looks up from his newspaper, but he folds it up and puts it down. He speaks quietly to Taylor.

DAN: Hang on a minute, ... Who said you get to tell me what to do? Who d'you think you are! Everyone in this game is scum including you. We're all scum, crackheads, murderers. No-one is better than the other, remember that, and don't tell me what to fucking do!

Taylor looks at Dan. Not in surprise, but with a half-smile on his face.

TAYLOR: Whooa now. Come on, temper temper. We can get into a little temper now can't we. We can all do that.

Taylor leans over to Dan and speaks quietly.

TAYLOR: Now just you remember who you're talking to, cos if you don't, we both know what can happen, now don't we......

Dan moves his chair away from Taylor.

DAN: No, I don't. Tell me. Tell me what can happen to me, cos I don't know.

Both men stare at each other for a few seconds and then Dan speaks.

DAN: I'm not gonna let you control me with this thing you know ... You're not gonna control my life because of what

Everyone knows it.

Jacqueline Panton

you know about me. Or at least what you think you know about me.

Taylor looks at Dan again with a half-smile.

TAYLOR: Oh, I do know what I know about you Dan, I do, and you can be sure about that. Your crackhead friend even knows the girl. He's the one who grassed you up.

DAN: There's nothing to grass me up about. She lied, she said she was eighteen. What d'you want me to do about that. How was I supposed to know?

TAYLOR: But we all know Dan, that you knew her father. You knew how old she was. You had to know. You knew but you didn't care.

Dan sits in silence for a minute, then he speaks.

DAN: Let me get this straight. I didn't know her father, and if she goes around tellin lies, then that's her lookout. I'm not gonna take a rap for somethin I didn't do. She's a liar!

Taylor leans on the railings and looks at Dan. He stands up straight again and speaks quietly.

TAYLOR: Whether she's a liar or not, it happened and you know what will happen if words gets out. I'm hopin it won't, but you have a part to play in that. If certain men in here found out, well …. You could cop it quite badly. I mean really badly.

Dan jumps to his feet and walks right up to Taylor.

Everyone knows it.

Jacqueline Panton

DAN: It won't work! I'm not scared of anyone in 'ere, no-one, not any of them and they won't believe you. Gary is a crackhead, a very dependant crackhead as well. Who would believe him anyway…… There're lots of ways to quiet a man like Gary.

Dan and Taylor stand in silence. They look at each other and say nothing. After a while, Dan sits down and covers his face with his hands. Taylor watches him as he sits there. He is stroking his beard when speaks softly.

TAYLOR: Look …. I think we know where we both stand. I'm not tryin to make things difficult 'ere, I just want to get on with it, get my share, and eh, everyone's a winner.

Dan is still sitting with his face in his hands. Taylor continues after about thirty seconds silence.

TAYLOR: I did try to warn you, when I told you how I felt about

Digo. He's a dog, he's racist and he's a bully. He bullies Bunny and Gary and he'll bully you if he can get to.

Dan still sits with his face in his hands. He is not looking at Taylor but he is listening to him, He continues to do this for the next ten minutes. When he finally looks up, Taylor has disappeared. He sits there for a while and then he stands up. As he goes to pickup his chair, he hears someone holla at him. He looks over the railings at the landing opposite and sees Mellow.

MELLOW: What's gwanin man, tell me, talk to me.

Everyone knows it.

Jacqueline Panton

Dan says nothing they just look at each other. Mellow hollas again.

MELLOW: What's up man …. Don't tell me nothin's wrong, I know you, what's up?

Dan is till standing there looking over at Mellow. Mellow starts walking over to him. When he reaches him, he says nothing, he touches him and motions for them to go into the cell. Dan lifts the chair and they both go into the cell. Mellow speaks quietly.

MELLOW: What's up man?

Dan is quiet for a while and then he speaks.

DAN: I swear I'm gonna do something really bad.

MELLOW: What d'you mean?

DAN: I swear …..

MELLOW: Come on man ….. talk.

Dan is quiet again for a few minutes and then he speaks.

DAN: Listen to me Mellow and, and listen very carefully….

He pauses for a few seconds, then continues.

DAN: You see that man Taylor, you see that man.

Everyone knows it.
Jacqueline Panton

Mellow is listening attentively as Dan pauses for a while before continuing.

DAN: Don't tell him anything you know.

He is quiet again for a minute.

MELLOW: Why? ….. come man tell me.

DAN: Don't tell him anything you hear or know. He's a fucking wanker man, a dangerous man, he will try to make man kill you.

MELLOW: Then, haven't I told you that all along man. Look what he did with me and Mac, he's a dog man …. Of course.

DAN: We need to watch our backs from now on. I don't trust any of them, not at all. I don't trust the one name Parks either. They're dangerous…… pass the word to Mac.

Mellow touches Dan as he turns to walk to the door. Whilst walking, he speaks.

MELLOW: You ain't tellin me everythin still…. But I'll talk to Mac.

Dan holds onto his arm as he walks away.

DAN: And oh, the one Gary, ….. leave him out for now.

Mellow stares at Dan for a while, then speaks.

MELLOW: Seeeene ….. I hear dat.

Everyone knows it.
Jacqueline Panton

He walks out of Dan's cell and half-closes the door behind him. Dan can be seen left standing in his cell. He slumps down on his bed and closes his eyes. Music can be heard in the background.

End of eighth scene.

Everyone knows it.
Jacqueline Panton

Scene 9

Mr Gepps is talking to Peter and Dan in the SO's office. He looks up at the door and manages to get a glimpse of Rush dashing away. Peter and Dan do not see Rush as they have their backs to the door. Mr Gepps does not tell them about the encounter.

DAN: I just wanna make sure we understand each other. That's my main thing here.

GEPPS: Of course…….. I'm right with that…….of course.

Gepps looks at Peter. Peter looks at Gepps but says nothing. Dan looks at Peter and continues.

DAN: We feel like ……….We feel like there's a lot of people onto this thing right now.

Gepps looks at the pair slowly nodding, then he speaks.

GEPPS: I hear that, but you shouldn't let other people and what they're doing get in the way of what you're doing.

DAN: I hear that, but I still think there are too many busy bodies in on it. They're all fighting against each other blocking and confronting each other.

Everyone knows it.

Jacqueline Panton

PETER: That's right. I've been in a few confrontations and I don't need any more.

Peter and Dan are quiet for about a minute. They sit there looking at Mr Gepps. Mr Gepps breaks the silence.

GEPPS: Guys I'm in control of this, you have to trust me. Everyone will get what they deserve. You put the work in, you reap the rewards.

DAN: We need rewards to reap, there'll be none left at this rate.

GEPPS: What d'you mean?

DAN: Everyone's handling the stuff and fighting against each other.

GEPPS: That's the way this things run though. It's not not above board is it.

The three men sit thinking in silence for a while. Then Dan speaks.

DAN: What does Digo think is going on?

GEPPS: He pretty much knows the score.....except about you that is. He doesn't know about you.

DAN: Let's leave it there then, he doesn't need to know. I don't like him.

The three men sit looking at each other for a brief moment, then Peter speaks.

Everyone knows it.

Jacqueline Panton

PETER: Well, I better be making tracks. I don't wanna be seen, y'know how it goes.

DAN: Me too. I've got enough on my plate. I'm watching everyone right now…..and they're watching me. Let's go.

Both men stand up and exit the office both scanning the landing as they do. Mr Gepps is left sitting in the office. He is about to use his radio when Doc pops his head around the door. Gepps freezes and stares at Doc. They both freeze for about a minute.

GEPPS: Good yeah?

There is silence for another minute.

GEPPS: What's up?

Doc moves his body slightly around the door. He looks suspiciously at Gepps.

DOC: Sceeene………..

GEPPS: What's up?

DOC: Sceene….. So that's how you're going on?

Gepps looks at him and speaks quietly.

GEPPS: Going on? Don't get you.

DOC: That's how you're movin then?

GEPPS: I don't know what you're talking about.

Everyone knows it.

Jacqueline Panton

DOC: You know what I'm talking about, I've just seen them coming out of here, they were talking to you. What's that about? Why were they talking to you?

Gepps remains seated as he speaks.

GEPPS: Look, just calm down alright! Let's talk about this without alerting the whole world.

DOC: Me….alert the whole world? I'ts you who's alerting the world.

GEPPS: For God sake come in and sit down. You hoggin up the door isn't helping anyone.

Doc slowly moves fully into the office, staring at Gepps as he does so.

DOC: I…..want to know what's going on.

Gepps motions with his hand for Doc to sit down.

GEPPS: Ok, just sit down ok? Let me explain. It's really nothing…..nothing to worry about.

Doc is still staring suspiciously at Gepps, he does not sit down.

DOC: It'd better not be anything to worry about for your sake really.

GEPPS: What d'you mean?

Everyone knows it.

Jacqueline Panton

DOC: You know what I mean….Parks was right about you….

GEPPS: Parks? What d'you mean?

Doc looks at Gepps keen interest to find out what was said about him. He turns his gaze away from Gepps.

DOC: You'll find out what I mean if things go wrong, and don't bother to ask me what I mean.

Doc quickly goes through the door pulling it behind him but not quite shutting it. Mr Gepps is left sitting in his chair with his mouth open. He is sat there looking at the door when it slowly begins to open again. He is curious and is about to stand up when Mellow pops his head round the door. They stare at each other.

GEPPS: What's happening?

Mellow stares at him for a while and says nothing. Gepps speaks again.

GEPPS: Come on man, what you staring at me for?

Mellow stares for a little while longer and then moves himself fully into the office looking out at the landing before half closing the door.

MELLOW: I had to check that Taylor wasn't in here first…..It's cool yeh?

GEPPS: Of course yeh….What's brought you here now?

Everyone knows it.

Jacqueline Panton

MELLOW: You know me, just checkin everythin out.

GEPPS: You're welcome.

There is silence for a minute or two and then Mellow speaks.

MELLOW: I was lookin for Doc. Have you seen him?

Gepps freezes and then catches himself.

GEPPS: Er....no I haven't

Mellow smiles slightly and then catches himself.

MELLOW: Oh, ok thought I saw him around

There is silence for a minute or two.

MELLOW: Ah…..well….alright then later.

He walks back to the half open door and exits leaving it still slightly ajar. About ten minutes later, Bunny enters the SOs office. He pushes the door with great force. Gepps feels a gush of wind sweep over his face Music can be heard from the wings. He sits still in his chair.

BUNNY: What are you gonna say now?

Gepps looks at him for a minute, then speaks.

GEPPS: What are you talkin about?

Everyone knows it.

Jacqueline Panton

Bunny looks at Gepps with squinted eyes for a couple of seconds.

BUNNY: You know what I'm talkin about. You fuckin know! You know what I'm talkin about. You've been at it all mornin, they've been pourin out of 'ere!

GEPPS: How d'you know?

BUNNY: Oh come on, you think I'm fuckin stupid? D'you think i'm fuckin stupid? Everyone knows what's going on, everyone!

GEPPS: I don't know what the fuck is wrong with you but you're getting on my nerves right now, you really are!

BUNNY: Fuckin Parks was right about you!

Just then they hear a knock on the office door. Both Gepps and Bunny stare at the door. Bunny becomes impatient.

BUNNY: Who the fuck's that?

The door slowly opens and Gary pops his head around it. Bunny explodes.

BUNNY: What the fuck do you want?

Gary freezes for a couple of seconds. It's obvious from his facial expression that he doesn't like the way Bunny is talking to him.

GARY: What d'you mean what the fuck do I want?

Everyone knows it.

Jacqueline Panton

Bunny shouts at the top of his voice.

BUNNY: WHAT THE FUCK D'YOUWANT? GET THE FUCK OUT!

Gary now steps right into the office and squares right up to Bunny.

GARY: What you gonna fuckin do about it? What you gonna do?

Bunny stares at Gary with a hardened facial expression.

GARY: Come on, do it! Come on, do it you fuckin cunt!

They square up to each other for about a minute. Bunny is staring directly into Gary's eyes. Gary realises Bunny is not backing down.

GARY: Stop talkin to me like a fuckin dog.

Bunny still stares at him hard, but says nothing. Gary slowly moves away from him and walks to the door. Before walking through the door, he looks behind him at Bunny and Gepps. They are silent. He walks through the door pulling it towards him but leaving it slightly ajar.

End of ninth scene.

Everyone knows it.

Jacqueline Panton

Scene 10

Rush is heading for the exercise yard. Whilst he is walking along the third landing, he sees Mrs Sharpe. He smiles broadly as he approaches her.

RUSH: Mrs Sharpe, I tried to send a message to you to let you know that I can't attend class.

Mrs Sharpe rests her A4 pad on the top of the railings and begins to write.

MRS SHARPE: Errr.. let me see, your class is this afternoon right?

RUSH: That's right.

She makes some notes on her note pad, ponders in thought for a minute and then speaks.

MRS SHARPE: Right... I'll pull out some work for you including these words you were trying to spell and don't worry about getting them wrong. What's important is that you make the effort.

Rush smiles as he thanks her and he is relieved that she was ok about him missing class. He caries on walking down the landing and heads for the stairs.

Everyone knows it.

Jacqueline Panton

Rush has just made his way down the stairs onto the second landing. He looks behind him and sees Mellow talking to Digo. Something is not right. He walks quietly over to them.

MELLOW: So what ya sayin?

Mellow is squaring up to Digo with a scowl on his face and his eyes squinted, he pushes Digo with his upper body. Digo pushes Mellow back with his own upper body and shouts in his face.

DIGO: Step away from me!

MELLOW: You a badman yeah?

Mellow punches digo causing him to take a few steps back into the landing door. The landing door is being opened from the other side. An officer enters the landing followed by a group of inmates from the exercise yard. Peter and Doc are among them. Just then, Mellow receives a punch to the head from behind. He has been rushed by Rush. He turns around quickly trying to steady himself, he sees Rush and they both start firing punches at each other. Rush gets the better of Mellow and knocks him to the floor. He then jumps on top of Mellow giving him heavy blow to the face with his fists. Mellow manages to throw him off, he gets back on his feet and sees Digo rushing towards him. Peter runs towards Digo before he reaches Mellow and punches him in the face. Digo falls to the floor on his back. All the men on the landing and some from the landings above, are shouting and cheering on the fight. Some of them are waving their arms in the air and making funny noises. A whistle is heard and the sound of officers rushing to the

Everyone knows it.

Jacqueline Panton

scene and shouting can be heard. Peter makes for the stairs but is quickly stopped by an officer who puts out his arm in front of him. Officers are now pouring onto the landing shouting; 'get behind your doors'. Men are scrambling everywhere. In the rush, two officers fall over each other and one is badly hurt, officers rush to his aid and try to lift him off the floor. Voices can be heard in the distance from other wings, the inmates are making monkey noises and shouting. Another whistle can be heard as more officers rush onto the landing. They are gabbing men as they bump into them. An officer grabs Mellow and pins him to the floor. Digo is still laying on the floor shouting to the upper landing; 'Watch out he's coming'. Rush races past the officers followed by Doc and about five more inmates. When they reach the top landing, Rush kicks a cell door that appeared to be closed. It opens. Two startled men jump to their feet, one of them is Gary and the other one is Bunny. Rush slowly walks towards Bunny whilst the other inmates stand behind the door. Bunny moves forward slightly as if to prevent himself getting trapped by the window. Rush immediately moves right into the space and head-butts Bunny on the forehead, bunny loses his balance and stumbles back into the window and the oranges that were stored on the window sill, can be heard hitting the floor one by one. The five inmates are now cheering Rush on in approval. Gary remains silent as he moves closer to the wall. He stands facing the guys with his back to the wall.

RUSH: Don't let me ask you for the shit. Where is it?

Bunny puts his hands over his face and receives blows to his hands from Rush. He falls to the ground and Rush jumps on top of him punching him in the face and head. Only the

Everyone knows it.

Jacqueline Panton

punches can be heard and suddenly bunny shouts 'Stop'. Rush stops punching him, he moves his hands away from his face. His face is covered in blood. The blood is on Rush's fists, Bunny's clothes, and also on the floor.

RUSH: Well?

Bunny looks at the five inmates with blood in his eyes.

INMATE 1 Don't try a fake location either.

Bunny motions for Rush to get off him. Rush gets up off him and stands over him. Bunny wipes his face with his hands.

BUNNY: Ok...Let me get it.

He reaches into his trouser and pulls out a small parcel that appeared to be taped to his leg. He looks at Rush and then at the other inmates, he then hands the parcel to Rush.

BUNNY: Here, here it is.

Rush inspects the parcel, he looks into Bunny's eyes as he feels and smells the parcel. He looks at Gary and at the other inmates who nod to him and each other in agreement.

RUSH: Alright.... good you know what's good for you.

He turns and looks hard at Gary, then back at Bunny. Bunny appears to nod at Rush, then there is silence for a minute. Rush now moves his face right up to Bunny's face.

RUSH: Where's the rest of it?

Everyone knows it.
Jacqueline Panton

There is silence for a while. Rush moves his face even closer.

BUNNY: It's under there.

RUSH: Where?

Rush looks at the bed.

BUNNY: It's under there, it's taped up.

Rush lifts the bed right up with the help of the other inmates and sees three parcels taped to the bed spring. He pulls the parcels which then detangles and separates into small blocks. The other inmates and Gary, all nod.

INMATE 2: Yeah yeah, that's it.

Rush inspects the blocks for a while. He then stuffs them back into their original wrappers. He then moves towards the cell door with the other inmates. One of the inmates pops his head out, commotion can still be heard.

INMATE 3: It's alright, it's alright.

The men then all rush out of the cell including Rush. Gary is left standing in the cell looking at Bunny. They stare at each other for a while and then Gary turns to the cell door, which is slightly ajar, and goes through it letting it shut behind him.

End of tenth sce

Everyone knows it.

Jacqueline Panton

Scene 11

The scene opens in the visits hall. The visits hall is big enough to fit ten tables that can each seat about 4 people. All of the tables are occupied with inmates and their girlfriends and their children. The hum of many voices can be heard as he inmates chatter to their visitors. Dan is sat at one of the tables with a woman called Gwen. Gwen is a known dealer and a casual girlfriend of a few of the officers and inmates in the prison.

DAN: Boy... I'm lucky to be on this visit, some mad ting happened yesterday. Mad tings.

GWEN: What, was there a fight?

DAN: Fight? It was more than that, it was mayhem. People Were everywhere, a lot of those guys are down the seg now.

GWEN: Poor bastards, they never learn do they.

As she speaks, she pushes a parcel under he table into Dan's hand. They carry on talking as this happens and they are not seen by any officers. Gwen is known as an expert with this kind of move. They continue to talk, laughing and joking with each other.

Everyone knows it.

Jacqueline Panton

DAN: Feels good.

GWEN: Oh it is good, only the best.

They are both quiet for about a minute. They sit there staring at each other. Dan smiles at her.

DAN: This feels superior.

GWEN: What does?

DAN: Getting it yourself, not having to wait on the crooked bastards to do it.

GWEN: Well this is it. You've gotta get there before them.

They smile at each other. They sit in silence for a couple of minutes. Their silence is interrupted by a voice coming from behind. Dan turns around to see Taylor.

TAYLOR: Well well well. If it isn't Gwen.

GWEN: Long time, how are you?

Taylor looks down at Dan.

TAYLOR: Will you excuse us for a minute.

Dan looks at his watch and frowns.

TAYLOR: You've only got fifteen minutes left, we can make up come on.

Everyone knows it.

Jacqueline Panton

Dan looks at Gwen, then looks around at the other inmates. He looks at Taylor, then at Gwen again and nods to her.

DAN: Oh alright then, fifteen minutes ain't gonna bite. But remember, fifteen minutes next time.

He gets up from the table, walks to the door, and is led out by an officer. Taylor looks at Gwen, and Gwen looks at Taylor without saying anything to each other. Taylor's gaze is fixed on her until he is seated in Dan's chair.

TAYLOR: Well well well........ It's been long time.

GWEN: It has hasn't it.

TAYLOR: And you're still lookin good.

They are both silent for a minute or two. They sit there looking at each other. Gwen breaks the ice.

GWEN: So how've you been then.

TAYLOR: I've been survivin in this place.

GWEN: That's a job in itself innit?

Taylor appears distracted by a thought and begins to scratch his beard.

TAYLOR: So err....... When last did you see Duffy?

Gwen look at Taylor as if he had asked a personal question. She looks briefly around the Visits Hall and then speaks.

Everyone knows it.
Jacqueline Panton

GWEN: Duffy? That's a blast from the past. I haven't seen him in ages.

Taylor sits looking at Gwen as he scratches his beard. He looks over towards the door in the Visits Hall, and sees Parks staring at him. He takes his gaze away from Parks and focusses on Gwen again.

TAYLOR: Are you sure about that? He's still around isn't he?

GWEN: Dunno.

TAYLOR: I could be wrong. Anyway, if you'll excuse me a bit I gotta see someone.

GWEN: Sure.

He gets up from the chair and walks away from the table. Gwen's eyes follows him over to the door where Parks is standing. She is puffing on a vape. Taylor is now talking to Parks.

TAYLOR: Fuckin bitch........ Lyin little toe-rag.

Parks looks at Taylor and shakes his head with a half-smile on his face.

PARKS: What did I tell you. You don't learn do ya. You will never get the truth out of scum-bag.

TAYLOR: Duffy said 'e'd give it to er. He did.

PARKS: Yes, but she won't give it to you will she.

Everyone knows it.
Jacqueline Panton

Taylor appears to be in thought for minute or two.

TAYLOR: You don't think she gave it to Dan do ya?

PARKS: What d'you think?

The two men stand there in silence for a while, Taylor squinting his eyes as he goes deep into thought.

End of eleventh scene

Everyone knows it.
Jacqueline Panton

Scene 12

The scene opens in the SOs office. The SO, Mr Carter, is sitting at his desk. He is looking through some reports on his desk. Digo is stood in the middle of the office propping himself up with a crutch to support his left leg. Carter motions for him to sit down on a chair near his desk. He sits with much instability.

MR CARTER: Well well well. These reports are pretty serious. I see a few familiar officers' names being mentioned. So you've come to check on what' been written. You want to make sure we've written what you've said.

DIGO: Correct.

MR CARTER: Right, now i've got Rush in the seg, Mellow in the seg, Paul Wright in the seg, Andre in the seg, and a few more. Not to mention Peter who has talked himself out of staying in the seg. I don't know what we're going to do about that one, tea-boy eavesdropper and god knows what else.

DIGO: He's much else.

MR CARTER: So are you sticking to the officers originally named.

DIGO: Absolutely, one hundred percent.

Everyone knows it.

Jacqueline Panton

MR CARTER: And the others......

DIGO: Yeh, the lot of 'em.

There is a knock on the office door, both men look towards the door and see Mr Gepps as he pops his head through the door. Digo immediately walks towards the door which is being blocked by Gepps.

DIGO: Step away from me!

Mr Gepps walks backwards out of the door followed by Digo.

MR GEPPS: Just a minute. Just a minute.

Digo continues to walk into Mr Gepps.

DIGO: Step out of my way!

They both stop moving.

MR GEPPS: Just one question.

DIGO: What's that?

Gepps lowers his voice and leans closer to Digo.

MR GEPPS: Why d'you name me?

DIGO: Cos I did! You're all the same. Fuck you!

Digo pushes past Mr Gepps and wobbles quickly along the landing. Gepps walks back into the office and sits in a chair

Everyone knows it.

Jacqueline Panton

near Carter's desk. They just sit there and look at each other for a couple of minutes.

MR CARTER: You know what this means don't you.

The room is quiet for a while. They both sit and stare at each other.

MR GEPPS: He'll be fired for sure.

MR CARTER: A bit more than that, and he has been warned. You know that. I keep on telling you guys, we need to set a good example for the people coming in to work in the prison service. We need to be proud of the establishment and our country. Officers should be upstanding, for want of a better word. We're working for the queen for fuck sake. If you set a bad exmple for the new guys, dealing and trickery, it'll all fall down. And we don't want that, do we?

Just then, the office door flies open and Peter marches in. He looks Gepps in the eye.

PETER: What the fuck is goin on! What the fuck is goin on! What the fuck.... How did Dan drop out?

MR GEPPS: Peter calm down, calm right down. I dunno!

Peter moves closer to Gepps. Mr Carter stands up and another officer enters the office and approaches Peter from behind.

Everyone knows it.

Jacqueline Panton

PETER: What d'you mean you dunno! Dan is dead and I should calm down? I want an answer!

Another officer enters the office and they both hold Peter by his arms. They force him to sit down on one of the chairs in the office. Peter slumps down in the chair almost breathless.

PETER: Everyone knows who they saw coming from downstairs just after it happened. He can't get away with it.

The two officers sit down beside Peter and start talking to him. Gepps is about to leave the office when Carter calls out to him.

MR CARTER: If you see Parks, tell him to come in here, without delay. Tell him it's urgent.

MR GEPPS: Sure.

As Gepps gets through the door, he bumps into Parks. He motions to Parks pointing his hand to the office door. Parks holds onto his hand as if to get him to give some information. Gepps pulls his hand away and walks off down the landing. As Parks enters the office, Mr Carter puts the phone down quickly and askes the officers to leave the room with Peter. Now alone with Mr Carter in the office, Parks quietly shuts the door. They both sit in silence for about five minutes and then the office door opens again. Three officers come in and two of them hold on to Parks in response to a nod from Carter.

PARKS: What? Is this it? I don't get a hearing?

Everyone knows it.
Jacqueline Panton

MR CARTER: You will remain at home under house arrest, until we send for you.

Carter nods to the officers again and they in response, walk Parks out of the office. Gary and Doc are on the landing. They see the officers escorting Parks.

GARY: You see that man there, he deserves everything he gets.

DOC: He's a bad man.

GARY: He had it coming to him, but he's so slimey, he gets away with things.

Gary stops talking and looks at doc. They both speak together.

DOC/GARY: Heard about Dan?

Neither man answers the other and they both speak together again.

DOC/GARY: He had it coming.

They stand in silence for a while as though no words were needed to express their thoughts.

GARY: He was two-faced, double-dealin and double-crossin.

DOC: I didn't like him, didn't like him at all. What happened?

Everyone knows it.

Jacqueline Panton

GARY: He double-crossed a certain officer. You don't do that.

DOC: What did he do?

GARY: Ah, some bird, I hear she gave him somethin that wasn't his.

DOC: What's new. This is what he does, he doesn't care. I heard about him long time from road.

GARY: She's got it comin to her as well though.

Gary quickly changes the subject.

GARY: So..... all the mandem in the seg.

Doc looks at Gary in thought for a while, then he responds.

DOC: Ummm......

GARY: Rush definitely got the tings down dere. Deffo, hundred percent.

Doc is silent as if to encourage more information.

GARY: He's got it and he stole from Mellow as well.

Doc remains silent as though not to interrupt the information flowing out.

GARY: He's a dog. All the one named Bunny, he should rot. I didn't feel sorry for 'im at all. You should have seen the blood drippin on the wing when they carried 'im out.

Everyone knows it.

Jacqueline Panton

DOC: Where did he go, which hospital?

GARY: I don't care where he went. E's always disrespected me, in more ways than one.

Both men stand in silence for a few minutes. They look at each other as if able to read each other's thoughts. They hear a tapping noise on the landing and they both turn around to see Digo. Digo is walking with a crutch. He has a swollen eye and a bust lip.

DOC: Yo, the bitch dead. Fucker.

Digo nods to Doc as he moves closer to the men. He finally stops and leans on the wall when he reaches them.

DIGO: The, rise and fall of a fucker. He went as hard as he came. They kicked him to death my mate heard it. Fucker. He was always takin people's food. And he could've been alright if he was straight.

DOC: Straight? What's that?

DIGO: He used to be well trusted by dem big man on road, but he double-crossed them. That's what he became known for but he double-crossed the wrong one this time. Good. Fuckin nonce.

Doc and Gary look at each other and nod.

DOC: I head about that, wasn't sure if it was true. Dutti-man.

Gary rubs his head and starts looking around the landing.

Everyone knows it.

Jacqueline Panton

GARY: Boy, I gotta make some tracks, business y'know.

He nods and walks away from the men.

DIGO: You see all that one named Gary, he's another fucker too. He's the one who set Bunny up, but dem same yout there will come back for him.

DOC: Parks's a bastard. They're all bastards. He won't get out of this one. Then again he probably will. He's on a suspension pending enquiry. We'll see.

DIGO: And Taylor?

Doc laughs as he tries to answer the question.

DOC: He's gone. He's a gonna man. He's still dangerous though, and that bitch better watch herself still. He doesn't forget, and he won't go alone.

DIGO: I know Gepps will keep his job, he always does.

DOC: Ah he knows too much. Carter can't touch him y'know.

DIGO: I fuckin hate them all and I know i've got to watch my back now, but I don't care. The best thing you can do in prison, is to keep a low, mind your own business, respect those who respect you, keep your fuckin mouth shut, do your bird and come out.

Both men are quiet for a couple of minutes. Then as if the words came from somewhere else and were not his own,

Everyone knows it.

Jacqueline Panton

Digo opens his mouth and gives life to them, with a distant look on his face.

DIGO: There'll always be plenty of food on road.

End of twelfth scene

Printed in Dunstable, United Kingdom